Apollo's Toy Box

Apollo's Toy Box

Ran Walker

Contents

Part Four

Part Five

Part Nine

Part Ten

Part Eleven

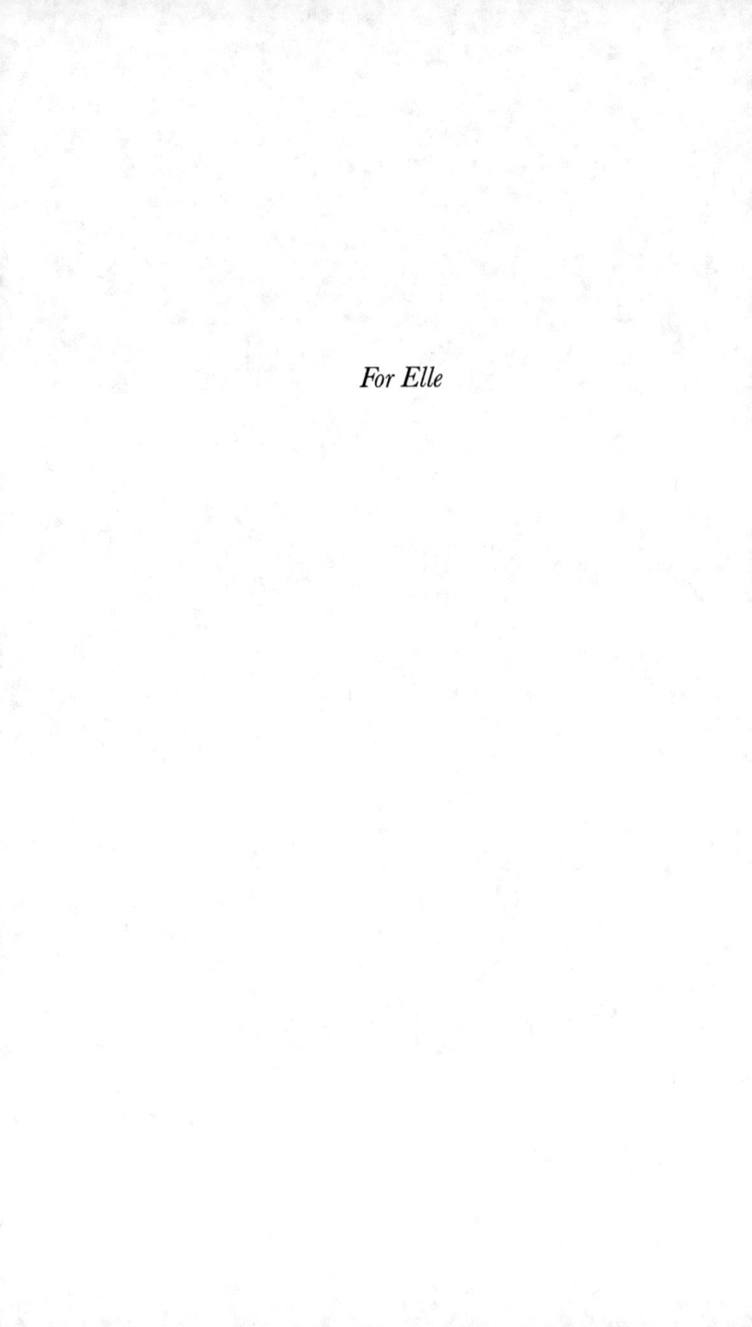

For Elle

There is no tomorrow.

— Apollo

Author's Note

Apollo — The Greek/Roman god who is said to be, among many things, the god of poetry

Apollo — A former heavyweight boxing champion whose life was cut short during an exhibition match with Ivan Drago

Apollo — A space program developed by NASA that ran from 1968-1972 and was responsible for putting the first men on the moon

Apollo — A theater in Harlem on 125th Street that has housed some of the greatest performers in human history

Part One

Grey

Even though he was American, he preferred the spelling "grey" over "gray," the latter, he imagined, being said with a relaxed jaw, the former with more of a fixed jaw. There was something a bit more dignified about the letter "e" than the letter "a," though he couldn't exactly articulate why. It was like raising a pinky finger when you sipped tea, as opposed to gripping the entire handle like you were holding a toothbrush—or something far less elegant.

The Labyrinth in My Attic

THERE IS a labyrinth in my attic, or so says my realtor (since I have been afraid to check). At night I hear footsteps zig-zag across the floor, and I wonder if those who are lost above me will ever find their way out.

Successful Relationships

Those two have apparently discovered the secret to a successful relationship: they break up every three months, wait three months, then reconnect. They say this keeps their relationship fresh.

We say it just delays their truly getting to know and understand each other, that the difficult parts are just as important as the easy parts. They tell my wife and me we are wrong and jaded by the ten years of our marriage.

Maybe they are right.

Her Birthday Present

Her father tells her he bought the orange shoes for her because they reflect the sunniness of her personality, even though she doesn't have that color in her wardrobe. He tells her it will be an accent when she wears neutral colors. Not even he wears this color, so she has deduced one of two possibilities: either that pair was the least expensive of the options available in the brand she'd asked for, or he's telling the truth. She chooses to believe the latter.

Chalkboards

By 2023 THE chalkboards in the old classroom were merely decorations, references to a distant past that did not include smart boards and computers. The custodians had long since given up checking for chalk dust on the ledge that ran along its base, the green of the boards functioning like wall art, something muted and soothing, yet hungry underneath, like Klein blue eager to burst through a layer of taupe.

The Reader
For James Joyce

HE HAS BEEN READING the same novel for over ten years now, but has yet to finish it. The eight hundred pages taunt him daily, as he finds himself rereading complete sections multiple times, not because he has found them so profound, but because he believes one has not read a thing until he completely understands it. One day he will finish the book, but even more, he will *understand* everything he has read.

Silver

SHE DIDN'T KNOW the exact moment when he became *old*. Although it must have been a gradual thing, it only dawned on her one day when she rubbed the hairs on his chest and noticed the silver strands sliding between her fingers. When she became aware of it, she suddenly noticed it everywhere: his eyebrows, interspersed in his mustache, between his thighs, even sprouting from his ears like some kind of metallic desert plant. The age difference hadn't seemed like much in the beginning, but now it felt like everything—and it took everything in her to not be afraid of the silver and to remind herself she dearly loved the man beneath it.

Armchair Critic

HE DRAWS asymmetrical geometrical figures with a ballpoint pen, his work simplistic, even childlike. Occasionally he does self-portraits, highlighting all of his imperfections, two-dimensionally, his blue ballpoint stabbing the paper until his art is viewable on both sides of the page. He has books and books of these drawings.

I am no scholar, but I suspect he might very well be the greatest artist of his generation.

Coltrane

HE IS LOST, like a pianist soloing on Coltrane's "Giant Steps." He knows vaguely where he is and what's going on, but she has left him and so he is lost, unable to keep up with the saxophone's perfection, just playing and counting the measures until the torture ends.

A New York Film

Even when he was in film school, he fantasized about making one of those artsy New York movies shot mostly at night during the winter, the snow layering the sidewalks like frosting on a cake, some soft acoustic jazz playing in the background, as the wide shot panned to reveal a couple cuddling beneath a street lamp, the large white, circular logo of a coffee shop seen clearly behind them. There would be no dialogue. The audience already knew this script, knew this moment. He would simply make it his own.

A Fable

THE KIDNAPPED WRITERS were each given a single pencil and instructed the duration of their lives would coincide directly with the lifespan of that pencil. If they elected not to use the pencil, they would remain imprisoned until their natural deaths.

At first the writers tried to ignore the pencils, instead attempting to share their stories orally. After a while, though, one writer's fingers began to twitch with yearning. He picked up his pencil and began to write. He wrote and wrote until the pencil was but a nub, and on the last day of the pencil's usefulness, one of the kidnappers came in and executed him.

This terrified many of the remaining writers at first, but then they became emboldened, understanding their words would live on.

When the group was finally down to one writer, the pencil became her only way out.

500 Shades

The human eye can discern over 500 different shades of gray, yet he still feels the need to distill everything to black and white. It is either this or that, no in between, no need for muddying the issue. It's about the simplification of choices, like walking into a box store and seeing two choices for toothpaste on the shelf. It doesn't matter that things are rarely so clear, but he abhors nuance, and he wants you to know that gray, as a matter of pragmatism, does not really exist. It's simply an illusion.

Brown Cookies in a Plastic Bag Getting Crushed by Libraries
After James Todd Smith

Sometimes he feels like an invisible man, his body internally bruised the color purple. This is what it feels like when things fall apart, he figures. This is what it feels like when you no longer have the love of your beloved.

He was a fledgling, coddled by his mama, day after day, so he never saw he would be on the street, dreaming about this Black girl dreaming, probably drinking coffee elsewhere.

The Missing Link

It was only after the great writer had passed away that an unpublished book was discovered among his papers that would have tied together all of the disparate novels he'd published during his lifetime into a single, cohesive, overarching narrative.

Miles Crushing Blue Cookies in a Plastic Bag
After James Todd Smith

MILES FROM HOME, feeling kind of blue, they got drunk off bitches brew, all the while trying to play it cool, their seven steps to heaven no better than the pencil used for sketches of Spain. Even with E.S.P. they had miles ahead of them, miles behind them, and miles around them, the trumpet's bell holding both the growl and the scream of their souls.

Americans

I SHOULDN'T BE surprised people still debate who wrote the Great American Novel when they spend so much time debating what constitutes being a true American.

Graduation

EVERYDAY THE STUDENTS assembled to take tests. All day long they took them. They were never told how they scored or given any feedback. Still, the tests continued to come, and the students continued to take them.

One day the tests stopped. The students were told some of them had graduated, while others had to remain behind to take more tests. Those who were left behind were joined by new students, and the testing continued.

Completely fed up, one of the students stood on his desk and declared he was done taking tests. For a moment everyone considered joining this protest, but the school's officers came in and took the kid away, never to be seen again, so the others quietly resumed their tests until it was their time to graduate, too.

Kara Walker

I AM HAUNTED by cartoonish caricatures of Black people, hiding in shadows, seeking retribution for centuries of subjugation, the subversive jigaboos and sambos, creeping, Massa dangling off the tip of a spear like a marshmallow yet to be toasted. And they will soon come for me, even though I have been them. They want to kill me so I, too, can be free.

Traditions

EVERY YEAR, the more rambunctious teens took to urinating on the headstone of Chester Willingham, a man who many villagers alleged was the pied piper who drowned half the children in the village centuries ago. In truth, Willingham was slain in a duel for the love of a woman who eventually left the village. The anecdote about the pied piper came up years later, probably an imaginative person joshing around with the locals, but as happens with many traditions, its origins didn't much matter, only that the kids could relieve themselves on Willingham's headstone with a clear conscious.

The Castle in the Corn

22

His neighbors poke fun at the fact he built a castle in his cornfield. They talk about how the castle is asymmetrical and uneven in parts (though this is intentional and indicative of many European castles). They talk about the fact he is not a serious farmer, because no serious farmer would waste crop acreage on something so frivolous. They say all of these things to make themselves feel better, less threatened, less aware of the bold beauty that towers above them in quiet majesty.

Christmas Lights

THEY SIT PEACEFULLY in the car, sipping hot cocoa from take-out coffee cups, listening to Vince Guaraldi play their favorite Christmas tunes, as the snow stretches beyond them through the Christmas lights lining the park. This view inside their toasty car is where the magic of the Christmas season resides. Outside the car, there is no magic, only the freezing cold and bulbs plugged into meandering power strips.

Gumbo

24

ONE SPOONFUL OF gumbo transported him back to his childhood, where his grandmother, always smelling of sweet oils, rubbed his back, as he lay across her lap, the hum of "Precious Lord" buzzing behind her closed, contented lips.

The Mundanity of Dreams

25

Sometimes she dreams of mundane things, like sitting on a folding chair in a room full of pennies, picking them up one by one and counting them. One time she dreamed she was counting threads in a tapestry. After these dreams, she wakes up calm and oddly refreshed, as the dreams in no way resemble the excitement of her actual job. But maybe that's the point.

Memories

HE IS GRADUALLY COMING to accept there are things he can no longer remember, but he wonders what this will mean going forward.

Will he forget when he proposed to his wife, as they stood in the clear waters of Aruba enjoying their first vacation in years? Will he forget the smell of his only son moments after the obstetrics nurse laid him upon his wife's breast? Will he forget the song he and his wife danced to on their 25th anniversary, the one that became their favorite many years ago when they dated in high school? Will he forget the taste of his favorite foods or favorite drinks? Will he forget the day he retired from teaching social studies and all of his former students threw a party for him with cake and fruit punch? Will he forget Christmases where he played Santa—and ones where he didn't? Will he forget the pain of burying his only child after a drunk driver claimed his life? Will he forget how his wife loved him through the worst of his days? Will he forget his family? Will he forget himself?

Death By Bibliophilia

ON THE DAY The Bibliophile died, it took half a day for the rescue team to climb the piles and piles of books that walled her inside of her house. There was no maze, no path, just books on top of books. When they finally reached her body, after moving thousands and thousands of books out into the yard to carve a path, they found her sitting in a chair, feet propped up on an ottoman, a massive hardcover book lying across her chest (so large some would posit it may have, in fact, suffocated her, presenting an immediate cause of death), her eyes closed as if she'd simply fallen asleep. As they took her away, one of the team members said, "Hoarding is a terrible way to go," as if that was any more a cause of death than the heavy book. The driver shook her head, though. "It's not hoarding if it's books."

Part Two

Pink

HER SHIRT and dungarees were splattered with red and white paint, Jackson Pollack-like, though the images on the canvas were as controlled as one side of a Kandinsky*. The colors blended into various shades of pink, figures taking shape, her imagination blushing with color like the cheeks of a boy discovering love for the first time.

---

* It is doubtful Wassily Kandinsky painted on both sides of the canvas at any point during his career; however, the idea of a two-sided Kandinsky (one side being chaos, the other being control) was a part of the stage play (as well as its film adaptation) *Six Degrees of Separation*, written by John Guare.

The Newness
After Erro

HE HAS NEVER HAD a girlfriend before, so he is quietly fascinated with every part of her body.

She allows him to adore her in this way, stroking the back of his head gently as he licks, then blows lightly across her neck.

In time he will learn how to please her, but right now he is taking in the newness of it all.

First Kiss

HE PULLS HER CLOSER, relishing the smell of her smoky, straightened hair, feeling the warmth of her curves beneath her big sister's dress. He does his best not to step on her feet, as they sway to The System's "Don't Disturb This Groove."

Out the corner of his eye, he sees the chaperones in conversation, and he knows this is the moment he should kiss her, but she surprises him by placing her head against his chest, a solace he didn't know he could provide, something more magical than a kiss, and instead, he places his lips gently against the cocoa buttered burn mark on the top of her ear, a scar that she bore for them to have this moment.

Timing in the Time of
Young Love

He longs to tell her how he feels, but he is afraid doing so would scare her away, so he counts the weeks until he can tell her the truth of his heart, hoping not to get the timing wrong.

Jaco

He plays the song on his bass, almost like a mistake, as if he is finding his way into the notes' beauty, his calloused fingers sliding over a fretless neck, all of this completely intentional, four strings plucked into total syncopation with his heartbeat.

He is attempting to play love.

St. Lucia
A Haiku

They lie by the shore, their brown bodies intertwined, a perfect pretzel.

Crush

SHE DOESN'T LIKE FOOTBALL, but in a small town, it is the place where people go on Friday nights, and she is hoping to see him, though he will not be on the field (he plays basketball), so she dresses in a cute pair of jeans she picked up in the mall one town over, her lipgloss the scent of bubble gum.

She is not looking for him to talk to her (that is too much for her to handle at this point). She just wants him to notice her, to think she's cute, and for his boys to tell him he should make a move.

He will be her first, she has decided, though right now that is too far in the future to dwell on. Right now, she just wants to stand out from the other sophomores and be someone a senior might be interested in.

Moments

AT NIGHT, they lay next to each other, whispering into the night. Neither was ready to take the next step, but with words like midnight caresses, they sensed it wouldn't be long. Until then, they would stare at each other, faces morphing with the imaginations that come from darkness, whispers carving the blackness into digestible moments of ecstasy.

Tupelo Dusk

THEY DANCE in the backyard with the sun setting behind them like the cliché of a book cover by an African author. The groove catches them, hooks them, and they are reeled in toward each other, the night tapping its microphone like, "Check one, check two," and soon they will be beneath a sky so clear they can see Venus and her funky little twinkle.

Downtown
A Tanka

Do you remember when I tasted you all night, and
your thighs swallowed me like the whale did Jonah,
and I slept in your belly?

Saturday Mourning

Her memories of him are trapped in certain fragrances and songs, the sunlight of a Saturday morning, the taste of Belgian milk chocolate, photographs she once snapped of his sleepy eyes. He lives on this way, and the days become a bit more bearable.

Love Expanse
A Haiku

THERE ARE times when he thinks he cannot love her more, and then it happens.

Afro-Boho Date Night

They will have a wonderful evening, eating lumpia they prepared together in their own kitchen. After dinner, he will massage her feet, as her moans take on familiar melodies. And the closest they will ever come to disagreeing is when they discuss whether The Foreign Exchange will drop another LP during this decade.

Heart

SHE'D BOUGHT a red pen and began drawing hearts all throughout one of her empty notebooks, attempting different styles on each one, but she found the simplest heart was the best. It became her stamp—her logo, if you will—like a Basquiat crown, and she used it on all of her pieces, whether canvas, poster board, wall, or notebook paper, and while others had done similar things before, none had quite captured the shape the way she had. Her level of focus rendered her incapable of drawing anything else of merit, but that was fine, since her fans wanted nothing more from her than her heart.

Who Am I to Judge?

I would find out years later my grandmother, a widow and head of the usher board, and Mr. Thomas, the widower from down the road who served on the deacon board, would meet up on her porch some Friday evenings and split a fifth of cognac while they told dirty jokes to each other all night.

Bottoms

46

He liked apple bottoms.

She liked red bottoms.

They found a common denominator, a peaceful way to coexist.

Now they both get what they want.

Elevators

ANDRE 3000 WAS NOT EVEN 20-years-old when he was lying on his back beneath a ceiling fan trying to catch the vibe for writing his rhymes. Now that I'm over forty, lying on my back beneath my own ceiling fan, I am thinking about all the rhymes I didn't spit, all the opportunities blown, all the inspiration I failed to recognize as inspiration, and I realize I have allowed my elevator to go down to the basement, where I got off and never got back on.

Plagiarized Love

ON THEIR THIRD DATE, he handed her a receipt indicating that he'd bought her the sun, the rain, the moon, the stars, and the mountains. She knew he couldn't buy her those things, but that wasn't what bothered her. What really got in her craw was he'd stolen the idea from an After 7 song.

The Day After

He can still feel his body pulsing, longing to be pressed against hers, the smell of her now absorbed into his pores, the memory of her movements, the sounds of the music that, like a bubble, have enclosed the moment into a perfect sphere, and he will carry her with him throughout his day, anticipating the moment when he can touch her again.

A Kiss on a Bridge

50

THEIR FIRST KISS takes place on a bridge at dusk, and she tastes the flavors of the spearmint gum he'd been chewing earlier. He holds her as if she is in danger of falling over a distant rail, but she is not, so she interprets this action as passion on his part. There is something safe about him, something signaling he wants to be in more moments of her life than just this one. She prays she is right.

Beneath the Mistletoe

At the Christmas party, he nervously approached her, a sprig of mistletoe hidden behind his back. When he reached her, she smiled at him. He took this as a cue to hold the mistletoe over their heads.

"Wow. Look where we happen to be standing," he managed.

She looked up at the mistletoe, then down at him. "You know mistletoe is a parasite, right?"

He shrugged. "What's that supposed to mean?"

"It means it leaches onto trees and takes from them without giving anything. It's a *taker*."

He nodded, pretending to understand all of this—but what he did manage to understand was that he was not going to get a kiss from her that day, or any other day for that matter.

Unintelligible

52

SHE WHISPERS something softly into his ear, but he can't make out the words, though he can sense the warmth from the closeness of her lips, the tickle of air implying a melody of some sort, something designed to blossom against his skin like an April sun piercing the coolness left by March, and he loves this feeling and, by extension, her, and he understands her words don't matter—not in the sense of being directly distinguishable—and with this comfort, he nods.

She Hates Love Poems

SHE HATES LOVE POEMS, but he loves to write them for her, an endless list of clichés, oftentimes using the same words over and over again, as if this recycling of imagery and banal vocabulary will make her feel closer to him, lubricate the possibility of exchanges between them, but she is bored with them, with him, because there is no love poem that hasn't already been written by someone far more talented than he, but she is open to a "like" poem or the occasional "infatuation" poem, something with fewer hyperboles and platitudes, and if that pans out, then they can talk about love, but not through poetry.

Purple
A Haiku

He could still taste the grape Now & Later she'd had earlier that day.

Secrets

56

THERE ARE things she told herself she would tell him when the time was right, but she knows the time will never be right, so she has decided not to tell him at all.

Part Three

100 Words to End the Debate

MANY DICTIONARIES WILL DEFINE *fiction* as a work of prose that contains made up elements. Nowhere in that definition does it talk about plot, conflict, and all of the other things we commonly associate with storytelling. Therefore, *fiction* is not necessarily synonymous with storytelling. To further compound this issue, consider the concept of a prose poem, defined as a poem (with all its accoutrement) written in the style of prose. As poems can contain elements of *fiction*, does that mean micro*fiction* can be prose poetry? And if so, why do we spend so much time arguing to the contrary?

Chasing Words

SOMETIMES THE WORDS come with ease, but other times he must chase down the bandit who has run off with them. Sometimes he can retrieve those words; other times, he watches as the bandit vanishes from view. He understands other words will come, but he still takes time to mourn the ones that got away.

Koalas

I AM FASCINATED BY KOALAS, these Australian tree-climbing marsupials that look like old men who just woke from a deep sleep. They parlay all day, munching on eucalyptus leaves, which are toxic as hell. This is the thing at the core of my fascination: this ability to consume poison continually, with no consequence. No animal wants to eat it. Their adults have few, if any, serious predators, so they can get old, just hanging out in trees, eating eucalyptus leaves, and parlaying. There's something beautiful about that.

Elephant and Castle

He'd had a pint (or three) in South London, and when he returned to the States, he'd had one in Boston, Chicago, Washington, and Seattle. They weren't the same, though. Too cold, and the footballer bit wasn't the same, not the same energy at all, no descendants of proper hooligans. But he did applauded them for trying—as if he were not a part of the *them*.

Victorians

She once read doctors held pocket mirrors against a person's nose to see if the steam of their breath would fog the lens. This was how doctors determined if a person was dead. For extra measure, they put a string in the casket, one attached to a bell outside of the burial site so if a person were to awaken in the ground, that person could pull the string and ring out an alarm to those above ground to begin digging. She thinks about this as she wanders through the Christmas Victorian village downtown. If she lived back then, the beautiful architecture would have been accompanied by these crude facts. It was far better to play Victorian than to actually be Victorian.

Patience

64

She had contemplated buying the arsenic for months, but when he died of a heart attack in his sleep, the purchase became unnecessary.

Invisible Problems

She walked in on her roommate making love to the invisible man from upstairs and immediately became jealous. It had not even been a week since their own relationship had ended, and here he was doing the inconceivable. She didn't know whether to be angry at her roommate or the invisible man. She almost made a scene, until she remembered the invisible man upstairs had an invisible brother and this was more than likely her roommate's sexual partner. It was, admittedly, difficult for her to tell the difference, especially in the dim light of the room, so she decided to go upstairs and find out for herself. For his sake, she hoped the invisible man was where he was supposed to be.

Anachronisms for Dummies

My cousin told me about a carving that had been found at an ancient burial site in Egypt. He claimed aliens had provided people with smartphones six thousand years ago, and the only reason they didn't use them was because there was no cellular network at the time. I mean, really, how do you argue with that?

The Guardian

THE GIRL MADE a doll of sticks and talked to it, imbuing it with a child's magic, and confessed to it her deepest fears, seeking its protection, and the doll, imbued with a child's magic, grew to the size of an adult and stood guard over the girl as she slept, ready and willing to stave off the evil that rested just beyond her bedroom door.

The Mandela Effect

THOUGH HE'D DONE ten films during his career, the director often found himself being approached in airports or cafes or conferences by fans of his first film, nearly all of them quoting the same line. On one level, he was flattered, but on the other, he was a bit disconcerted, as that line (or anything remotely close to it) never appeared in that film—or any of his others.

The Clarinetist

Before she became a world-famous clarinetist, she was once a little girl with split reeds and dexterity issues, who squeaked so badly her parents considered soundproofing her bedroom. Now, thanks to her, there are millions more kids picking up clarinets and taking the painful steps toward making beautiful music, too.

Glorious Dome

THE THICK, curly hair coming out from beneath his fedora was not intended to be a tease, but, as his wife would later relate of their first date, his baldness on top had come as more than a surprise.

Split Vision

SHE MEANT TO CHECK THE "YES" box on his love letter, but her decision to "look pretty" without her progressive lenses left her to the whims of fate.

Old School

72

He was a man of his generation, or at least that's what they liked to say when he talked of things now politically incorrect. He made off-colored comments about things that struck him as bizarre, unconcerned with whether or not his words slapped or bruised people too young to identify with him. They'd never stood up to anyone, peppered their knuckles with the blood of a knucklehead who talked too much. No. This generation was soft, as far as he was concerned. Fake gangsters shooting because they couldn't throw a left hook. He couldn't care less they thought him out of touch. They were the strange ones, not he, and they could take their sensitive feelings and flaccid vocabulary with them. He was built different, and he wanted everyone to know.

Kernels

AT TIMES, he would start writing a story only to find he'd lost it, that kernel of magic that flickered briefly when he began, but was apparently destined for no more than a few words. Stories required more magic than a kernel, even the tiniest of stories.

Climax

She'd never had an orgasm with him during the forty years of their marriage, so the steady build between her thighs was a first, and she planned to enjoy it. She yielded to her inhibitions, allowing herself to perform, her body a whirlwind of movement, her reverse cowboy immaculate, the tension feverish. She heard him emit a deep gasp, withered hands falling away from her soft waist, and she closed her eyes. He called to her, but she did not respond, and in moments his body lay still, his erection stronger than ever, and she climaxed, going in and out of time, savoring a moment a long time coming. He'd once promised he'd give her an orgasm one day, even if it killed him. He was a man of his word.

Likeness

75

As THE ACTOR began to lose control of his physical and mental faculties, the studio exercised its AI rights to digitally plug him into their blockbusters. Soon enough, his fans fell in love with these new movies, and when he eventually died, hardly anyone noticed.

The Failure of Language

76

HE UNDERSTOOD how language could betray you, how unclear it could be. He didn't identify as Black, couldn't identify as Caucasian, and thought biracial was too ambiguous, as it didn't speak to the specifics of his identity. But language could be like that sometimes.

Drowning

He believes, with every fiber of his being, that he can drink all of the water in the ocean. This is the thought he will focus on.

Freak

SHE WOKE and brushed her teeth, while they watched. Once she finished, she quietly dressed in the shadows of the open closet doors, then turned around to wave at the people on the other side of the glass.

The children screamed, and the adults comforted them.

She quickly did a cartwheel and jig, and the children, now delighted, applauded. Relieved, she went about her day, as they watched, pointing at her and whispering to each other, all for the price of admission.

The Swimmer

Some nights when she looks up at the star-filled sky, she imagines she can bounce, as if from the swimming pool floor, and swim up into the sky, where she would backstroke among the constellations and into infinity.

Happy Tales

She told me everything shouldn't be so dark, that not every tale should be twisted, so I tried to write a story with a happy ending, where people sang and danced in flower-filled fields and the sun never set—but eventually they grew tired and lay on the scorched earth, their limbs exhausted, and the vultures began to circle overhead, and through parched, cracked lips, these people begged for me to bring it all to an end, so I did.

Black Santa

The woman on Fox News says Santa Claus is white, but none of the Santa figurines her mother has placed around the house are white.

The Item He Loaned Her

He couldn't believe his neighbor was being buried with an item he had loaned her. He'd pled with her for years to return the item, and she'd always promised she would, but then something would happen to prolong her holding on to it. That she had left notes in her will to be buried with this item, this thing that was his and not hers, rankled him, so he attended her funeral, and when it came time to view the body, he grabbed the item out of the casket and held it above his head and said, "Mine," then exited the church before all hell could break loose.

Student Loans

THEY SAT at the back of the classroom, pretending to study, their phones positioned just beneath their desks. Whatever was going on outside the room was far more interesting than what was going on inside of it.

In the future, though, they would be unable to remember a single thing about the course (or what had been going on outside of it), as they paid their student loans off, one slow month at a time.

Part Four

Ten Horrible Reincarnations
(and Counting)

He was reincarnated as a roach four times and a spider six times, and each time his wife would smash him to death with the soles of her shoes, leaving his innards splayed across the wall, floor, table, or wherever he had the misfortune of being noticed. He wanted only to tell her he loved her, missed her, but his karma did not allow for him to do that. Instead he was destined to keep coming back as something she hated, leaving her with the idea the house had some kind of infestation as opposed to a husband desperately trying to reconnect with his wife.

The Tooth Fairy

THE KIDS USED their money to buy candy.

The candy they bought rotted their teeth.

They placed their rotten teeth beneath their pillows.

The old woman then took the rotten teeth and left behind more money for more candy for more rotten teeth, until she had enough of these rotten children's teeth to fill in the atrophied sockets of her mangled gums.

The Hand

IN THE NIGHT, as she bathes by candlelight, she sometimes feels a hand rise up between her thighs and massage her. She knows she should be afraid, but she has grown rather fond of this unknown hand caressing her. Though she cannot see beneath the surface of the water, she knows it is there, her own hands gripping the edges of the tub, trembling from both fear and ecstasy, not yet ready to know the truth, praying for amnesia once she is satisfied and only the water around her body remains.

Liminal Space

A FAMILY once lived in this place.

Layers of dust cover the curio cabinet so it blends seamlessly with the wallpaper, all of the broken plates hidden inside, a fractured spine of china propped against a surface smoothed with spackle and drywall. There is no evidence of the boot that once crashed through like a battering ram. The table is small and chipped, pocked with anger and the residue of pain.

Mattresses dangle from bedsprings like bodies after a blast, memories muted like a dying man's whispers. This place holds both heaven and hell, like fraternal twins, their parents trying to love both equally but failing. Nothing embedded in this fabric but time.

The shotgun rests in the corner, propped up, sanctimonious, its position an afterthought of an over-caffeinated coroner who had to tiptoe through a nightmare. Now all is silent, and emptiness hunts from room to room like an archfiend licking its chops, hurling itself ever towards its prey.

Sometimes it's hard to remember a family once lived in this place.

The Trees Along the Property Line

AT FIRST SHE didn't notice. She'd rarely used the backyard in the beginning, but now that she'd started a small garden there, she felt the dimensions of the yard were changing on her.

She decided to measure the distance from the trees along her property line to the garden, and over the course of a month, she noticed the distance had closed by an inch.

Surely, she was mistaken in her earlier measurement, so she tried the experiment again. It was an inch the second time, which meant the trees had moved two inches in two months. Was it possible for trees to move, or was there something else going on?

She called out tree specialists who told her such a thing was impossible given the time period. But the surveyor confirmed what she'd expected. The trees were encroaching upon the house.

Because the present plot of land didn't align with the property deed, she found herself unable to sell the property, and just as she prepared to leave the house and take the loss, a root shot up through the floor, grabbed hold of her ankles, and pulled her down through the floor, deep into the earth.

The trees gradually receded, the property regaining its original size, and her estate had no problem selling the house to another eager first-time homeowner, one who might or might not notice there was something not quite right about the trees along the property line.

Cuthbert

He is fixated on octogenarian necrophiliacs, particularly those in small towns, where few antebellum houses remain, places where Southern culture sputters in asthmatic breaths and frayed Confederate flags hang from dirt-caked pickups, where people use the title "Miss" with an air of disdain for the unmarried, and in the heart of this place, the people will bend over backward to accommodate their monsters, for fear there will be no one to return the favor when it is their turn.

The Scream Queen

THE DIRECTOR UNDERSTANDS there is an art to the perfect horror movie scream. Few can do it well, which is why he has employed S to do voiceovers on each of his films. Her screams are bloodcurdling, disturbing in the best meaning of the word. He wonders if S is screaming from a place of trauma, but the question will never be asked. He senses he will never sleep again if he knows the truth.

Storytime

ONE MORNING DURING PLAYTIME, the kindergarten teacher assembled the children from their block-building and coloring and told them adults had it all wrong about children and what they could and could not understand.

"Remember the three pigs?" she asked.

They nodded in unison.

"Which is more believable: that pigs built houses or that the wolf ate all of the pigs?"

One child raised his hand and replied he'd liked the pig who built the house of bricks.

"There is no such thing as a pig who can build a house, but there are millions of instances of a wolf devouring other animals."

"Animals like dogs?" another child asked.

"Animals like humans," the teacher replied.

The Phone Call

97

She holds the phone in her trembling hands. She's read an urban legend about this before, but like many things born of the Internet, someone has taken this nightmare of 1s and 0s and placed it upstairs in her darkened house, perhaps in a closet or beneath a bed, the evil now a game for some sadistic monster, whose breathless voice announces again that he is in her house.

We Miss You

She awakens to roaches crawling across her stomach, their antennae tickling her skin. She wants to scream but fears one might enter her mouth. Shaking her head to keep them from her face, she feels them in her hair. Somehow these tiny creatures have found her in her suburban mansion, miles from that tiny, unkempt apartment of her youth, their tiny legs now roaming her bedsheets, covering her like a thick, insufferable comforter, refusing to let her escape.

Chased

Every night he had the same dream: a large, savage beast chased him through the forest until he was finally able to elude it—or wake up. He wondered what would happen if the beast ever caught him, if such a thing might kill him in his sleep. Assuming he were to wake from the dream, would he bear the psychological scars of one who had been mauled? Would he enter his next dream encased in those wounds? He did not know. The only way to avoid having to find out the answers to those questions was to stay ahead of the beast, which is what he had every intention of doing.

Vampirism

She loves to nibble on his neck until it bleeds, the salty, coppery taste of him smearing across her eager lips. He moans, pretending to enjoy it. She will top him off later, he knows, but first she must draw blood, taste him, a few drops to wet the tip of her tongue, and he will feel like the prey of a seductive predator, and she will smile her devilish grin and kiss him with his own blood on her tongue. Then she will make love to him in the most transcendent way, his blood clotting beneath his own sweat.

A Theory of Monsters and Other Humans

THE HORRORS of her mind did not include the supernatural. There were no vampires, were-wolves, zombies, aliens, sea creatures, or Love-craftian monsters. There were no possessions, demonic or otherwise. There were no ghosts dwelling in the liminal spaces of decaying Southern gothic country houses. There were no special concocted agents that could be ingested to make one transform into something inhuman. There were no natural or unnatural disfigurements of the human body. No. The horrors of her mind included only one simple thing: people. The evil at the heart of man, this Hobbesian horror, was far more terrifying than any reasonable individual could stand, and she found this horror alone to be the most disturbing of all.

Business Trip

SHE BELIEVES no one will be able to tell what she has done. She pretends to be herself, the normal soccer mom of two, the pleasant, churchgoing wife whose husband is away on business in India. She doesn't know hold long this lie will hold, but she will deny—even under oath—knowing what happened to him.

The Butcher

THREE YEARS INTO THE PLAGUE, people who bought meat from the butcher refused to ask where he got it. The fact it wasn't tainted was enough for them.

Clawed

She awakens to the breath of the beast, its claws piercing the flesh of her stomach, digging. It wants her to yield, but she can't. Instead, she summons a lifelessness, and her tormentor, satisfied, crawls back into the city's darkness. The call she makes afterwards will save her life, but the keloid scars that mark this nightmare will remain, like Morse Code, a constant reminder of her distress, her fear, her determination to survive the unsurvivable.

Jump Scare

They scream a cacophonic chord when he springs from the closet, one quickly regaining her senses and running, the other stuck, holding her note too long, as if her brain can only do this one thing until he has completely silenced her.

Detour

THE NEW APP led him into the neighborhood. He had no way of knowing others like him had taken this same route—had been lured—and this neighborhood, flush with its swirling blue lights, would never allow him to reach his destination.

Scary Stories

The kids took turns telling scary stories to each other around the camp fire. Like insect repellent, the stories actually scared away the monsters that would have otherwise crept in and consumed them.

Darkness Follows

Darkness enjoys following the children around the house, easing into corners, behind doors, under bunkbeds, its belly pressed against the floor, and when the lights go out at bedtime, it spreads itself like a blanket across the ceiling to watch them sleep.

Trench Coats

The students laughed at the trench coats, cracking jokes at the kids crazy enough to wear them in the warm temperature. But this was high school and people did a lot of unusual things to express themselves, to feel comfortable in their own skins, so it quickly became unremarkable. After a while, everyone simply got used to seeing them, these kids in their trench coats, and no one ever considered what a coat that length might one day conceal.

Contagion

She sneezes the thick, green mucus into the handkerchief and neatly folds it into the cloth, the green barely visible. She is tempted to dispose of it, but fears someone else might come upon the infection and it spread even faster, so she tucks it into her purse, careful to steer clear of any crowds, hoping such a measure might prevent what she senses is inevitable.

One Note

The child only plays one note on the piano. It's a low D that moans, and the child is persistent, hitting it slowly, an ache of apprehension like the beginning of Madonna's "Live to Tell," and memories of Christopher Walken and Sean Penn and guns and blood and nighttime and that damn D droning in the background like the hum of a man about to die. And the child plays it over and over with the monotony of a Gregorian chant, this hauntingly precocious child unable to play anything else. And I want to beg him to play any other note, provide any other resolution, but the child is determined to drown me with this note, as if I were a rat blindly following the seductive sounds of the piper's Zauberflöte.

Dark Stories

SHE WANTED to write the kind of children's book someone would eventually concoct a dark conspiracy around. That conspiracy theory would then take on a life of its own and haunt adults to no end (like Paul McCartney's car crash in 1966[*]), while the children for whom the work was assumably written would delight in the beauty and magic of it all, oblivious to such adult nonsense.

---

[*] If you're too young to know about this urban legend, simply do an internet search for "Paul Is Dead." That's a rabbit hole you will get lost in.

Monster Logic

SHE DOES NOT BELIEVE in *monster* monsters. To her, all monsters are human, but not all humans are monsters, though it is not always easy to discern which is which, mainly because monsters who are human often behave as normal humans. That's how they cause the most damage, she observes. So she is on the lookout for humans who are normal humans, not monsters, although she understands there is a chance, albeit a small one, the humans she believes are normal humans are really monsters.

Part Five

Punctuations

THE STUDENT always used hearts in her punctuations: periods, colons, ellipses, tops of semi-colons, the bottoms of exclamation points. There was something playful about it, but the teacher insisted the student be more professional and write the marks correctly. It was only after he gave her that instruction that he noticed a small bit of the magic she'd brought to the class was now completely diminished.

Dreams of Laughter

IN HIS DREAMS he was a comedian. Every night he killed it. Ironically, though, when he was awake, he didn't care much for comedy and couldn't tell a joke to save his life. Instead, he was a police detective, where there wasn't much use for a skillset involving punchlines. The word "kill" took on a very different meaning here. But he had to admit it felt good to go out on stage, if only in his dreams, and take on the crowd, a group of strangers, and make them laugh until they fell out of their seats.

Final Cut

He bought all of his favorite movies on DVD just to have access to the bloopers and deleted scenes. He learned much more about what made a movie special by seeing what failed to make the final cut.

The Final Wish

SHE DOES NOT RECOGNIZE the face in the mirror, her dishwater blonde replaced with thick black locs, her skin now a deep bronze, her once blue eyes now as brown and as deep as a fairytale forest. This new beauty transfixes her, but she struggles to reconcile who she believes herself to be with what she actually sees, wondering how she will navigate the world now. This was her wish, though. No more pretending.

Sole Survivor

When they discovered him, barely alive, on the deserted island, he'd told them he'd survived on only fish and plants, but there'd been no fish nor plants.

He vowed he would never tell anyone what he'd actually eaten to stay alive. It was better to keep that to himself.

Allow Me to Break Your Heart

SHE MADE a series of one-minute black and white films, none of them with dialogue, all of them about loss. She premiered them in the back of a small pub in San Francisco, where the eclectic audience watched in silence as she broke their hearts into a million pieces, one by one.

The Warrior

THERE IS something unsettling about the way she lumbers with the axe hoisted onto her thick shoulders, her calloused feet dragging along the forrest bed like tattered teddybears being pulled by toddlers. She has slain more men than she will ever admit. That is part of being a warrior, she will say. But what she will not reveal is how much she enjoyed it.

Rain

SHE FELT it was pointless to complain about the rain. Natives of London didn't bother, nor did natives of Seattle. The gloomy overcast came with the territory. And there was something tranquil, something oddly beautiful about the absence of sun on a regular day, the need to illuminate oneself from within to make that magical thing happen.

Sweatpants

THE GIRLS SAT in small groups at the edge of the cafeteria watching the jocks walk by in their gray sweatpants. Some of the girls would point and whisper, all of them making inferences from what they could scarcely make out beneath untucked t-shirts. Yvette didn't understand why this was something her friends enjoyed doing, and no one thought to take the time to explain to her what this particular sport was all about.

Amoransia

HE KNOWS she will never desire him in a reciprocal way, and this idea makes him smile, *Urkel-ish*, because he is, if anything, tenacious, aching to have his heart peppered with noes, not unlike a novelist papering the walls of his office with a litany of rejection letters from agents and publishers alike. He chews on unrequitedness like a gum that will never lose its flavor.

Personal Uniform

127

FOR A YEAR he wore the same outfit every day. The point was to make a fashion statement, but as is wont to happen with these kinds of things, no one seemed to notice, let alone care.

Longevity

Five scores earlier, when she was a child, her father gave her three pieces of advice on how to live a long, prosperous life. She can no longer remember them, but she figures she must have followed them to a "T."

A Black Male Writer Questions Publishing

WHAT DID publishers expect from a Black male writer?

Had things improved since he read of Monk's exploits in *Erasure* or Kamal's experiences in *White Pages*?

Was he destined to write a version of Blackness for a majority who understood little of his experiences, preferring simplicity over nuance, while championing their willingness to be more diverse?

Would they even know how to market his book, or would he be left to carry the entire burden himself?

Was it possible the only person he could trust to tell his story authentically was himself?

Was it better to publish the book himself?

Was he overthinking all of this and telling himself what he wanted to hear?

Was he afraid?

Was he right?

Was there any way to really know the answers to any of these questions?

Scenes in Afrosurrealism

I AM that off-kilter scene from the movie where you know some weird shit is about to go down 'cause you can hear the swelling horns of Minnie Riperton's "Les Fleur" building up in the background like a nut about to get busted, and those of us who like that *Twilight Zone* shit sit up in our seats and say, "Yes!" or "Bring it, Lakeith!" and Blerds glow like freshly shaved domes, and the celebration of being seen and felt resonates like light from a star a billion miles away.

The Deal

THE MONSTER under my bed and I have made a deal. He will sleep in my bed, go to school, do my homework, eat Mom's Brussels sprouts, and do my chores. I will sleep under the bed and read comic books all day with a flashlight. He's such a sucker.

The Teddy Bear

She had learned to get to sleep without it, but occasionally the teddy bear would climb down off her shelf and crawl into bed next to her, for old time's sake.

The Man of Her Dreams

In his dream, someone had insulted his wife, and he felt the need to defend her honor. He was not one for fisticuffs, but he threw a right that connected with the guy's nose, then began ramming the guy's face against a brick wall. Something felt odd, though, as the man seemed unfazed. It was then that he knew he had to kill the guy before the guy killed him. The knife appeared from the places convenient things in dreams appear, and he swiped it across the man's throat. It was only as he pulled back the blade that he asked himself, "Am I the kind of man who would kill another man for insulting his wife?" With the answer lying before him, he woke to his wife sleeping soundly beside him, unaware of what he would do to protect her honor, wondering if such a horrifying reality was worth sharing.

Addiction

She constantly warns her grandfather to cut back on his smoking; her grandfather constantly warns her about staring at her smartphone all day.

The Cheerleader

She was disturbed when she heard stories of women her age masquerading as teenage cheerleaders her daughter's age. What gave a person the audacity to think forty years of living could be disguised in the taut, young skin of a child? That element was the most troubling, not the fact the mother's teen daughter had been tied up in a basement while the mother lived her daughter's life. That part was irrelevant. She was only bothered by the thing for which she was the most envious. Daughter be damned.

Who's Afraid of the Dark?

THOUGH, in the back of his ten-year-old mind, he knew the suit jacket on the hanger was nothing more, when the lights went out, the coat seemed to fill with a nightmarish presence that loomed over him as he slept.

The Pugilist

Although he had long ago retired, men still feared him. He moved about the room like a ferocious beast that was known only for the carnage it left in its wake. Even the way his head swiveled on his shoulders and his eyes, feral-like, hunted people moving about his periphery were the thing of nightmares. He looked like the kind of animal an idiot might try to pet, only to have his hand remain behind, locked in the jaws of this predator, the prey's flailing wrist, punctuating the folly of such a thing, splattering its deep crimson everywhere.

Up Through the Toilet

THE FIRST TIME IT HAPPENED, it caught her off guard, the massive rat meandering its thick body up through the base of the toilet bowl, splashing deliriously, its wet fur brushing against her bare ass. How she managed to hop off and close the lid before the rodent got the run of the bathroom was beyond her. The flush worked, but the situation left the unsettling fear it could recur. And she was right. It would happen again, sometimes after heavy rains, but she was ready, always looking down as she sat, hand resting on the toilet's handle, legs never completely relaxed, always ready to stand and do what needed to be done.

Messy Woman, the Invisible Superhero

IN HER DREAMS she found she could go invisible at will. She used this superpower to lurk around, spying on others, looking into their personal lives, exploring their secrets. When she woke, she found herself craving these powers, and because she couldn't simply snoop around unnoticed, she decided others were deliberately withholding their secrets from her.

The Novella-ist

SHE FANCIED HERSELF A NOVELLA-IST, a name she'd coined when she learned no one had cared enough to create a monicker for those who'd written books slightly shorter than novel-length. It had started with a handful of short stories that were a bit longer than she'd originally anticipated, but it quickly evolved into her trimming the fat from would-be novels she started, honing them into something that felt tighter, leaner, and easier to both write and digest.

She created a social media page for others to share in her passion, but the idea of a "novella-ist" just never caught on. She gradually began to understand there were few, if any writers, who would strictly commit to this form when full-length novels rested just beyond *them thar hills*, a place where publishers casually walked about plucking plump books from bountiful trees.

Cultural Debates

THE COUPLE DEBATED the second season of *The Wire*, the last season of *The Sopranos*, the last season of *Game of Thrones*, and the third season of *Atlanta*, their back and forth mirroring debates within The Culture, this feeling that either the shows had somehow "jumped the shark" or in some way had managed to be so brilliant as to be misunderstood by casual fans.

Part Six

Older

SHE'D PICKED him up at a bar down the street from the campus. He was virile and their lovemaking had been vigorous. Like a trophy catch, he was destined to be tossed back into the sea, neither of them worse for the wear. But he wanted to see her again. Rather than relent, she told him she was twenty years his senior, and he quietly left her alone. She rarely told young men the truth, unless, like this one, they forced her to.

Tacenda

Sometimes as they ran their lines, an eerie feeling would come over her and she would remember he had served a seven-year stint in prison for voluntary manslaughter, all of this while she was finishing her MFA at Yale. He was now a famous actor—far more famous than she—and the world seemed to have moved on from his indiscretion in a manner that seemed to suggest nothing had ever happened.

The Train

I am resting on the 4 train, eyes closed, coasting peacefully down the east side of Manhattan, being rocked gently by the slight sway of the car, uninterrupted in my slumber by the occasional stops of this express train. I am going downtown, but I am dreaming about turning into a giant and walking out into the Atlantic Ocean and towering over Lady Liberty, tiny whales swimming around my toes.

I awaken with a start to a woman saying "munchin' house" then "mind the gap," and I open my eyes to a different car, my eyes barely catching the words "Mansion House" through the scuffed window. I do not know where I am going, but I exit at Tower Hill and emerge to the familiar scent of urine, concrete, and street food.

I am not home, yet I am home. And the train continues on without me.

Horror Movies

He loved horror movies, but he was bored by most of them. The way he saw it, the handful he absolutely adored were so good they made up for the lion's share that were either overly cliché, uninteresting, corny, or just not scary. He eagerly anticipated the October horror movie lineups, though, as sifting through the chafe was as much a time honored tradition as was putting up a Christmas tree in early November.

Insomnia

SHE WILL NOT TELL her husband the source of her insomnia, the reason she eases out of bed during the night, wrapping a blanket around herself as she sits in a chair by the window. Its because she can still smell charred flesh, feel the scorching heat of inferno-like flames, and her guilt weighs on her like a battleship anchor, as she remembers holding the lighter in one hand and the aerosol can in the other. She'd heard about it at school, and it was meant to be an experiment, not take the life of her brother and a first responder. So she sits by this window, this now grown woman, alert and upright, wanting to protect her family from the first signs of danger, sometimes wondering if that danger is herself.

Bad Weather

She hated short stories that started with the weather, but it wasn't because it was cliché. Her father had given her a pillow of Snoopy sitting at a typewriter, typing Sir Edward George Earle Bulwer-Lytton's famous "dark and stormy night" bit. Those were some of her fondest memories of him before he became sick. Now, she found the line difficult to read and writers who started their short stories with references to the weather a bit depressing.

Forgotten

While sorting through some boxes of old college notebooks her mother had set aside for her, she came across a peculiar love letter from a man she couldn't remember. His penmanship was almost feminine, his words poetic and fierce, full of passion in a way that should have made him more remarkable and able to withstand time.

Now she wondered how he was doing, and if he ever found someone to whom such words might prove perfectly placed, someone who would not just hold on to his words, but remember him as well.

Books About Books

SHE IS that reader who will pick up any novel dealing with bookstores or protagonists who are writers or stories set where a real life writer has been fictionalized. It doesn't matter if the story is a romance or a mystery, she loves books and those who write them, and although her literary agent has warned her against writing books like this because there is an over-saturation of these manuscripts at publishing houses, she is helpless to abide by this advice. She must write what she loves and pray someone will publish her book and give other readers a chance to have the feeling she so deeply cherishes.

Oh Shit

He stared at the text.

"Did you mean to send this to me?"

It was only then that he noticed he'd sent the text message to his boss and not his wife.

The Luxury of Luxury

HE HAD A PORSCHE PANEMERA, but he didn't like taking it out in public for fear someone might lean on it, park near it, or even breathe on it wrong.

He had a limited edition Montblanc Meisterstuck fountain pen, but he never carried it with him for fear someone might ask to use it or it might fall out of his pocket at the most inopportune time.

He owned a pair of Off-White x Jordan 1 Chicagos, but he never wore them because he didn't want their value to decrease or for their fragile construction to get snagged on any manner of things the streets could produce.

Instead, he drove a Ford Focus, carried Bics in his pockets, and wore Crocs, saving the other things strictly for his social media posts.

Chicago
A Haiku

The hawk snatches her back erect like a straightedge, January jolt.

Visible

THIS HALLOWEEN, he will dress as a clown and stand under trees that line the street of a suburban neighborhood. He will carry candies in his pockets and offer them to children. Parents will steer their little ones away from him. They will call in sightings of him to the police. He will be a menace by merely standing there in his face paint. Every other day of the year he is invisible, but tonight he will be seen.

Whispering

THE CHILDREN WHISPER his name for fear he will hear them and appear to them and chase them until their legs cramp with exhaustion and they curl themselves into a ball to fend off the snapping of his razor-sharp teeth.

The Macuto Line

IN CÉSAR AIRA'S novella *The Literary Conference*, his protagonist talks about each person reading various books and developing a knowledge peculiar to that individual, meaning some puzzles can only be solved by one who has read a particular set of books and through those books, explored the vast, diverse elements at the core of the puzzle.

This author writes his book, wondering—hoping—the reader will possess the potpourri of knowledge necessary to appreciate what is there, but if Aira is right, there will only be one who does.

Hits and Hashtags

HE DIDN'T CARE much for the music, but it broke his heart that his daughter had to mourn so many of her favorite rappers.

Spit

Miss Beatrice (pronounced evenly as bee-at-triss) keeps a spittoon fashioned from an empty baby wipes tube she uses to spit snuff into. The kids she babysits say her breath smells like raisins, and they laugh with childish disgust when she spits a wad of tobacco juice into the canister, before closing it and placing it back on the small table beside the couch. Soon her stories will be on and the children will be down for their nap and her spittoon will be full.

Gone Fishing

T HEY STAND on the pier every Friday morning, their lines cast into the deep, waiting. Some days they catch something they can actually keep, while other times they are there just for the companionship. Since their retirements, their wives have encouraged them to get out of the house, so this is their weekly playdate, the place where two grown men have been sent by their wives to do something other than sleep and watch television.

Ironies of Poor Prognosticators

Although his YouTube channel had amassed over 600,000 subscribers, who tuned in every week to watch his ASMR sneaker unboxing videos, he couldn't shake how much time he'd spent in the principal's office for talking too loudly in class.

Lethologica

His lethologica was a well-known part of his personality, those around him often trying to suggest words when his mind drew its usual blank, their recommendations often missing the mark, but it was still better than the dead silence of him standing there, finger raised like a lightning rod, reaching for a word he knew but could not, for some indiscernible reason, pull from that ethereal plane above his head to rest on his tongue.

The Literacy of Fish

WHEN SHE WAS EIGHT, she told her friends she had taught her goldfish to read, but no one believed her. That likely had everything to do with the fact that, as a general rule, fish could not read, not to mention the fact she was widely known for her limited bouts with veracity.

Memories

"WE DID IT A LOT. LIKE *A LOT*," she said, as if that was all she could remember of their relationship years later.

Complimentary Insults

"How many times have I told you to clean this room," his father said. "It looks like modern art up in here!"

He was unsure how to take that statement. Part of him believed it to be a compliment, like he could make a killing in the art world if he just put his mind to it.

But he knew better.

Neptune

EMERGING FROM THE BLUE, he raises his trident in triumph, the frost of its distant orbit lying before him like loyal subjects, bodies bowed.

Miles Davis

HE WISHES he could say he learned about Miles Davis's *Kind of Blue* from his father, who was more of a Motown man, but the truth was he saw a Clint Eastwood movie, where he caught glimpse of the album cover while hearing the music playing on the soundtrack in the background.

Crash

THE BLACK BOX on the plane revealed all 250 passengers, along with the crew, were singing "Ring Around the Rosie," in unison, moments before the plane went down.

Part Seven

Life Lessons

HE SITS across from his grandfather, his tiny feet dangling in the air. The old man takes a deep draw on his cigarette, taps the ash onto the vinyl card table, next to the ashtray, then grabs a can of beer with his free hand. The little boy watches his grandfather's Adam's apple bob up and down, as the sound of the Budweiser rushes down his throat like river rapids racing across rocks. The old man points at the boy's cards, then the boy, who is now cowering in his seat. *Don't play that card again*, the old man warns, and the boy nods, pretending to understand.

Sleep Is the Cousin of Death

174

To GET to sleep each night, he imagines his bed is a cloud and that he will fall through the floating droplets, his body flailing in space as it hurtles toward the ground like a boulder dropped from the top of the Empire State Building, the impact destined to render him unconscious.

Be

SHE IS afraid to use the word "be" because Black people sometimes use that word in ways the textbook doesn't allow, and she doesn't want the teacher to look at her and say she has misused the word "be" or her use of the word is tied to BVE and therefore tainted by the powers that be, be they folks like the teacher or folks who want to act like the teacher, so she conjugates the verb, dances and shimmies away from the straight up "be" that be bugging the hell out of her.

Harlem
A Haiku

Despite the concrete that surrounds her, she tiptoes through fields of daisies.

Blue

The sand is hot underfoot, so she sprints toward the shoreline, relishing the coolness of the ocean enveloping her toes and the earth sliding beneath her heels. The foam pulls back, leaving her exposed for a moment, then rushes back, tickling her ankles like a thousand tiny feathers.

Ndoa ya Marekani
A Haiku

SHE SPOKE English at home because it was the only language he knew.

Simple

DEEP DOWN, he feels he doesn't deserve her, that a woman like her is too good for a simple man like himself. She could be the muse for a great artist who would create masterpieces in her likeness that would be praised by future generations, but instead she has lowered herself to walk the path of this Earth with him.

He will cherish her and try to make her feel a fraction of what she might have felt with another, always praying his best is enough.

Dreams
A Haiku

She feels her dreams are clichés of clichés, but she dreams them anyway.

Bad Art

He loves bad art. The worse, the better. Few things are more inspiring than a bad movie or a bad book or a bad song, because in his creative mind, bad art leaves the artist with this thought: surely I can create something better than this, and that seed of an idea can do more for him than experiencing great art, which sometimes has the opposite effect, because it's hard to compete with greatness. So, he relishes bad art, finding in it a comfort that allows him to create, even when it seems his creative well has run dry.

Transatlantic
A Haiku

THE WATER SCARES ME.

My ancestors wave to me from the deep, dark depths.

The Transmogrification

ONE DAY she will begin to write novels again and focus on expanding each of her ideas beyond poems or fictional ditties. She will patiently explore the souls of these ideas and transform herself into this new animal that blends in with all other animals and walk the perimeter of this holding pen, and she will seek their approval and measure herself against these peers and judge herself by the lofty dreams she has adopted, and she will see this as a type of success that is more important than what she has already created when words mattered more than book sales.

The Magical Negro Exodus

His filmography is filled with "Magical Negro" roles, and while he was aware he'd done a few, he was flabbergasted to learn he'd done so many. He had never taken seriously the idea of being type-casted when paying rent and having food to eat were greater priorities, but now he understands Hollywood sees him as this one thing.

Is it too late to be anything other than this? Surely there is a script that could help him break out of this—or maybe a bit of magic he could conjure to save *himself* this time around.

Novices, Circa 1987

THEY MEET behind the her house, the July night giving them cover, and they whisper things to each other neither will remember years later, but in that moment, feeling so much in love, they try to kiss, tongues touching, attempting to ignore Uncle Junior's TV blasting *Wheel of Fortune* and Big Mama talking loudly on the corded landline in the kitchen.

Loneliness
A Tanka

SHE WILL TAKE him home so she will not be alone, and in the darkness, she will ask him to hold her and to pretend he loves her.

Forgiveness

HE WONDERS how many of his mistakes as a teenager could have been attributed to a still-developing pre-frontal cortex. At that time, his mistakes felt excusable because there was plenty of life ahead of him. Now there are not so many years in the distance, and he finds himself reflecting over his youth, painfully aware of those decisions, as if somehow turning back the hands of time and doing right by the people he hurt would somehow make the world better. But he also understands those mistakes have brought him to this point in his life and that his path may have been *different* had he actually navigated those experiences *differently*.

Maybe it was his pre-frontal cortex; maybe it was that he was simply an asshole. Either way, he must make his peace with this past and forgive himself so he can be present for the gifts of life that still remain.

The Earthling

HE KEEPS a picture of the Earth—the first one taken from space—on his office wall. When the damn feels like it's going to burst, he looks at this picture and reminds himself there is much more going on than his immediate concerns, that he is on a giant floating ball spinning around one of the billions of starts out there, that things only have the meaning that he chooses to prescribe to them, that his job is not the whole of who he is or what he is—or what anyone is—and a peace settles over him, as he simply relishes being an Earthling.

Lessons for the Young
Caped One
A Tanka

There is plenty of sky from which to fall if you're a superhero who has failed to understand your power comes from within.

Mother's Notebook

THEY FOUND the notebook buried within the bookshelf between two hardbacks. In it, the ideas their mother could never arrange into an intelligible book. Words stacked upon words, the cursive neat, but heavy.

It could have been a book, they thought.

It should have been a book, they thought.

Genius

She is more perplexed by her prize-winning poem than the people who have alleged to have loved it.

42

Jackie Robinson Day for a Yankees fan is confusing if you're a brother rocking the 42, representing for the culture and you get confused for a brother sporting a Mariano Rivera jersey, which is not the worst thing in the world, especially since he helped us win five World Series championships and became the first player to ever go into the Hall of Fame unanimously (a distinction that should've gone to The Kid), but you're standing there representing Jackie, still thinking about Sandman and his loving up on Trump (which is his prerogative, but not the look you, personally, want), and the 42 feels different, and you realize the fans of other teams don't have this quandary, and for a moment you envy them, but you love your pinstripes, and it's Jackie Robinson Day, so you focus on that and that alone.

Journaling

SHE TRIES to write something everyday, shed some part of her soul onto the page, in hopes that this act will allow her to tap into a part of her imagination that has not yet revealed itself to her.

Warning

Everything gives her gas, she warns him, and to be with her, he must embrace that side of her, and he, stunned by her beauty and sense of humor, welcomes the whole of her, and has never enjoyed the full smell of her perfume, uninterrupted, ever since.

Their Song

His BEST FRIEND reports to him his ex, who just married someone in their extended friendship network, used *their* song in her wedding, and he is beside himself, remembering how they had come to embrace that song, a song that now belongs to her and a new person, and he is left pondering if anything is sacred anymore and wonders if her new husband will ever be original in any way.

Mama's Gun

ON SATURDAYS in September she strolls through the winding paths of the park, Erykah Badu nestled in her ears, songs harkening back to memories of a summer where she felt the first true moments of independence, an internship that invited her to explore her own unique perspective of the world, and while years have since passed, the feeling of freedom remains and Badu sings they won't be naming no buildings after her.

Sky
A Haiku

THEY KNOW I CAN FLY. My wicked crossover
breaks the legs of eagles.

Part Eight

Pennies
A Haiku

THERE ARE SO many wishes at the bottom of the well, forgotten.

Chagall

MAYBE ONE DAY, when he is in his nineties, he will return from a day of writing in his studio, have a peaceful dinner with his wife, then take a seat in his favorite chair and leave the world behind.

The Quest for Forgiveness
A Haiku

HE TRIES to outrun a past that refuses to let go of his legs.

A Change of Perspective

THAT BLUE DOT THERE? That was us—or who we used to be when we stood still, the Earth moving around us, and we puffed out our chests like we were the masters of the universe, little He-Men laughing at our dominion, ultimately failing everyone and everything until we had to forever change our perspective.

It looks so tiny, doesn't it? It makes you almost want to return.

Almost.

Too Hot, Too Cold

IN THE SUMMER, the classroom is hot from a turned-up thermostat, although the heat outside is nearly unbearable; in the winter, the classroom is cold, from a turned-down thermostat, although there is ice on the ground. The students try not to laugh at this recurring theme and instead have compassion for a person whose job must be incredibly difficult to do.

Crook in Her Neck

She sleeps on the sofa and awakens with a crook in her neck, and she walks around campus, massaging the area between her shoulder blades with a free hand, and guys offer to give her a massage, though she knows they have little interest in helping her remove the crook.

Laidback

207

He is laidback like J. Cole in tube socks pulled from a bag of six, like Minnie Riperton's lazy afternoon, unflappable, no wings, just chilling in time and space, no rush, no need to be anything other than here.

Ghost

THIS POEM DIED at its inception, not because it failed on a structural level (as there is no real structure), but because it was a poem that never found a subject other than itself, but since it was nonexistent anyway, so then was the subject of this poem, so it was indeed destined to fail, and, truthfully, we are now simply seeing its ghost.

Friday Night
A Haiku

WATER WASHES the week from her skin, as worries swirl around the drain.

The Little Ones

THE LITTLE ONES close their eyes and cup their hands together, imagining they are eating a burger and that it will fill their growling stomachs.

The Origins of Originality

He will write and write and write, and one day he will notice his pen leans in a specific direction, his notebook rotates just so, his words stack in such a way that what he is building now has a specific look to it, and he will sit back in awe that all of this happened without his knowing and that he has somehow, some way, managed to develop the thing writers crave the most: a style.

Island

SHE SMELLS like mangoes and vanilla, and he longs to lie in the shade of her, tasting her fruit.

The Bluesman

THE STRINGS SCREAM in his dreams, melodies seeking to fill the gap left in the groove of the sheets, a single strand of hair all that remains of love fueled by passion and rotgut, the pillow now cold and stale, his memories a useless artifact, and she may as well be on the moon since she is not here with him, but at least he has his guitar, the one that would never abandon him.

Crumbling Castles

THE CASTLE IS much cooler than he anticipated, but not cool as in dope; cool as in cold. The rooms are adorned with things that reflect a period of time in which the word "boring" did not exist, the staircase, without a railing, narrow and spiraling up to the battlements, where a banner flies. In his mind, there was a poetry to this, but now, gazing out beyond the former dominion of this kingdom, he is quietly relieved he did not have to live through this era of history.

It's Hotter Than...
A Tanka

THE SUN WEIGHS on them like some cliche about heat that leaves us laughing, wild Southern hyperboles that will offer little shade.

Longhand
A Haiku

She writes the letters so they line up perfectly and become the poem.

The Best Magic Trick

THERE'S a mirror in the box that makes it look like he's disappeared. This is his best magic trick. He's so good at it he sometimes refuses to come out from behind the mirror, having convinced himself that disappearing leaves behind a wonder that can't be achieved by being present.

A Poet's Story

Drunk off autumns of acid jazz, debating whether to dread my hair before it met its undeniable fate of male pattern baldness, I put pen to page, not yet understanding the power of words, instead treating them like toys to be manipulated for entertainment, getting digits from someone who knew less about poetry than I, though my eyes would eventually open and the words would take on new meaning, rhythms opening up like my mind digesting a Dilla beat, and here we are: bald, beautiful, believing in the power of poetry, determined to sing the soul's infinite songs.

Guilt

HE READ EVERYTHING SHE WROTE, though he didn't like much of it. It wasn't that he thought she was a poor writer—the potential was clearly there—but the content simply failed to interest him, and because of his guilt from being a white man reading a Black woman, he felt his dislike of her work was possibly a byproduct of his own background, so he kept reading her work in hopes of either finding something that struck a chord in him or him changing enough in his thinking he was able to better relate to her subject matter.

Four

220

THAT NIGHT, he will lie awake in bed, thinking about his team lined up, fourth and goal, four seconds left on the clock in the fourth quarter, down by four, and how the ball hit him dead in his palms before bouncing into the hands of the safety covering him.

Interlocked

221

HE HOLDS her hand until he can no longer feel his own fingers. At this point, he is only psychologically aware they are touching.

He wonders what this means.

Ice Cream

222

HE IS TEMPTED to lick the ice cream running down his fingers from an overstuffed waffle cone, but he has been taught that kind of thing is in poor taste, so he watches it drip from his fingers to the ground, where, clearly, it cannot be enjoyed by anyone.

Mollusk
A Haiku

SHE WON'T COME out of her shell, afraid of what waits for her in the world.

Fame

224

SHE FILMS herself and watches herself online and wonders why others don't watch her, too, because she is entertaining and has things to say and feels she is also deserving of fame.

The Stories We Tell Ourselves

Part of his legend was he'd written his first novel on a series of fast-food restaurant napkins in a single caffeine-infused week, using a pencil worn down like Andy Dufresne's rock hammer, but the truth was far less glamorous, that he'd simply sat at his computer and taken two years of writing and stopping and writing and starting over and writing and doubting himself and writing because the idea wouldn't go away. The napkin thing? That was just doodling.

Part Nine

The Hypnagogic Emcee

SOME NIGHTS I freestyle in my sleep, and I can flow infinitely. Every word is at my disposal. I am beyond merely rhyming words and elevated to syllabic rhythms. I might very well be the best emcee to ever do it, and all along I have been keeping this lyrical mastery to myself, like some kind of secret power best broken out only when Thanos starts trippin' and trying to snap*, so I sit on this ability, thinking if the world new this, they'd lose their shit. Then I wake up and am incapable of spitting even eight straight bars that aren't strained, wondering where my vocabulary went, where my skills went, and in that moment, I am humbled, a mere mortal again, not even interested in rocking a mic —but there's still a part of me that wonders if anyone will ever be as good as I am when I'm asleep.

---

* Yep. That Thanos from the MCU.

Generation X Boys

DURING THE SUMMERS, they watched *Reading Rainbow*, then rode their bikes to the public library to check out LeVar's recommendations, hoping to put a notch on their reading lists so they could earn a personal pan pizza from Pizza Hut's BOOK IT! program.

Lazy afternoons playing outside, these miniature scientists mixed things to see what would happen, saving their Icee cups (since they looked like robots) and fashioning together stripped pipe cleaners to make wires that pulsed with electric imagination.

At night, they slept beneath a large sheet clipped to a box fan, and made Transformer and Darth Vader voices until they went to sleep.

Spring
A Haiku

THE SONGS of Spring call to me like arcane whispers from beyond my dreams.

Upon Watching "The Wiz" for the Umpteenth Time, Part 1

EVILLENE, the Wicked Witch of the West, was allergic to water, so that means she probably didn't bathe, which means she was likely pretty funky (not in the George Clinton sense either, unless one thinks he might be funky in a similar way), and she had the heat in that room cranked up, and we all know funk and heat don't mix well, and those munchkin slaves had to be musty, too, since they were around someone who was allergic to water, so they were hotboxing funk in that red ass room up until the moment Dorothy and company came through, liberating munchkins and giving them a shower strong enough they literally came up out of their skins, dancing damn near naked as they rejoiced in freedom from tyranny, echoed by a tremendous amount of funk that lay in piles on the floor.

Denim

HANDS STAINED WITH INDIGO DYE, he hangs the cotton strips on a line, where the blue will gradually lighten, and the fabric will be woven into denim and eventually fashioned into jeans that are destined to be superior to jeans made anywhere else in the world, and while he understands there are many others who make selvedge jeans, he prefers to be recognized for his work in creating the blue cotton strips that lay at the foundation of this masterpiece.

Misplaced

She has read the poem ten times now and is still confused.

Her favorite poet has written a poem with a misplaced modifier in it, and while confusion could naturally stem from the grammatical meaning of a phrase, her confusion does not lie there; it lies in whether or not the poet intended to use a misplaced modifier as some kind of poetic device.

Maybe the following phrase was meant to suggest a double entendre of sorts:

A guy in a jacket missing one eye

Is the guy missing one eye, or is the jacket missing one eye? Can jackets have eyes?

On the surface, it appears to be a classic example of a misplaced modifier, but she respects the poet so much she wants it to be more than that, more than a mistake, perhaps some kind of literary genius that up to this point has evaded everyone.

Upon Watching "The Wiz" for the Umpteenth Time, Part 2

IN *THE WIZ*, the Tin Man's fourth wife was named Teeny, but there was nothing teeny about her.

The Wild, Wild '80s

During the '80s, our commercials wanted us to be civilized and sophisticated, whether it was through our choice of deodorant or our choice of Dijon mustard. It's actually ironic, though, when you consider Gen X latchkey kids running amok, bicycles leaping plywood held up by milk crates, wildness all around us, Boomers testing out adulthood, but all of this could be tamed with a few advertisements. It's almost comical when you think about it that way.

Cookin'

THEY STAND IN A CIRCLE, heads nodding to the beat looping through the speakers. One by one, they will drop sixteen bars into the cypher like chefs, each contributing an ingredient to the pot they will share once they have finished. They will keep this scrumptious meal strictly to themselves.

Sampled

A LITTLE KID WHISTLES A TUNE, and a songwriter hears it and acknowledges how catchy it is, so she writes a song with that melody, and a singer hears that song and wants to cover it, and eventually an emcee hears that version of the song and samples it, and one day the little kid who originally whistled the tune hears it on the radio and wonders why the melody sounds so familiar, never once realizing it is his own.

Black Matter

or A Moment in Time

HE MISSES her in the quiet moments of night, when the city sleeps just beyond his window sill. The electric glow of downtown hums the melody of her moans, and he smiles, remembering her like he would a favorite song playing on the radio at the most unexpected moment.

Does she think of him anymore, or has the world shrunk her memories of him into a footnote of her heart?

The only thing they now share is yesterday, a yesterday that struggles to echo into the present, except, at least for him, when the night, like a cinematic screen, beckons him, city soundtrack pulsing in the background, reminding him of when only the two of them mattered.

Nothings
A Haiku

SHE WHISPERS NOTHINGS.

He wants them to be sweet, but they will never be.

Impressions

He begins to speak his adoration, but she shushes him.

Don't ruin it, she whispers.

So he must keep this mounting ecstasy tucked inside the shadows of his mind, lest he spoil the moment.

Tatlock
After Ralph Ellison

Some days I sit and wonder what ever happened to Tatlock after he kicked all that ass to take home $10, after he nursed the bruises of Black fists and volts of electricity, his mind still etched with the nude form of a woman he would never see again, after he woke up from nightmares of men screaming their hate at him, after he handed over that money to his mother, his contribution to a household in need of far more than his body could give.

99

A Haiku

He's been told books sell better when the penny is kidnapped, held hostage.

The Sky Is Not Blue

I KNOW the sky is not blue, although it looks that way to me.

Some days I wonder if my limited perceptions will eventually come back to haunt me, or will I be wise enough, when the time comes, to know to shift my perspective?

I know only that the sky is not blue. Still, I can't help thinking how blue it looks to me.

Astronaut
A Tanka

He is lost in the space between them, galaxies and stars and black holes.

He longs to get home to her, breathe her atmosphere again.

Prose Poetry #1
A Haiku

SHE SAID line breaks are overrated—but *she's* known for writing fiction.

Horror Novel

Every October she tells herself she will write a horror novel, but horror is a challenging genre for her. She appreciates it too much to simply write down random ideas. Plus, there is a plethora of bad horror already out there, and if she is going to do this, it has to be a valiant attempt, one that might even be classified as above average.

But what to write?

She is not a fan of possession movies or aliens. Not because they are too scary; they are not scary enough. She wants something that is terrifying in a manner few have ever seen, and because she has no idea what that is, she has not written a thing.

Year in, year out, she tells herself she will write a horror novel, but she may have to simply accept she is too afraid to write one.

On Rainbows

THE SPRAY of the hot water pulses between his shoulder blades, and he remembers the touch of her fingernails dancing along the hairs of his chest, and later the hum of her voice in his ear as she pressed her chest against his. His body now aches to be touched—loved—like that again, and he wonders what he could have done differently to keep her, but sometimes people want different things in life, no matter their chemistry of intimacy.

Sometimes a rainbow is just a rainbow, and there is no pot of gold at the end, no matter how badly he might've wanted one to be.

Tasting Autumn

IF AUTUMN WERE A WINE, I would drink it slowly, swishing it around my mouth, savoring its flavor, nose deep in some sophisticated stemware, falling in love with its vintage, admiring its legs, swirling it around, doing my best imitation of an oenophile, just to let it know I appreciated it and wanted to live inside it until it was no more.

Political Stickers

WHILE DROPPING my daughter off at school, I pull up behind a minivan covered in political stickers.

Our kids will likely sit next to each other in class, and all the while neither will think about these politics until one day they'll be forced to.

Holby

A Haiku for THW

HE WEARS ONLY BLACK BECAUSE, for a Black man,
life is its own protest.

The Weight of the World

252

Some days it feels as though the world is leaning on the outer walls of her room, the pressure causing everything inside to groan with exhaustion, and it is not that she doesn't want to go outside. She simply can't.

Indubitably

He used the word as a test to determine if he'd been drinking a little too much. The scale worked like this: if he could say the word three times in quick succession, then he knew he was relatively sober by all accounts. If he tripped up at any point along the way, he knew it was time to turn over his keys and call a cab.

It never occurred to him saying the word over and over could make it easier to say, thereby giving himself a false sense of sobriety. Having had this pointed out to him by a fellow colleague from the university, he decided to change his word every time he went out for drinks, rather than abandon his test altogether.

Part Ten

Bumper Stickers

THE STICKMAN HUMPING THE WORD "IT" is automatically assumed to represent the phrase "fuck it."

As an armchair grammarian, though, I see the phrase "fucking it," which clearly doesn't have the same effect.

Books Galore

The books in her bookcase cause the shelves to bow like Mississippi chicken legs on skinny Black boys, calves high and tight like naps, and one day she will either need to reinforce the shelves or let them collapse beneath the weight of pages read/being read/to be read, but that decision will not be made today or tomorrow or the next day, and not because she's trifling; it's just that she has yet to create a priority that supersedes reading the books themselves.

Meeting the Parents

IT WAS an apology by way of introduction, which he had explained as a mixture of energy drinks over the past three hours and the lack of suitable restrooms once they'd left the interstate and he'd had no intention of making such a mess of their bathroom, but the force of his bladder caused him to momentarily lose his balance, and therefore his aim, and he was indeed grateful to meet them and his love for their daughter was, in fact, genuine, despite the unfortunate, aforementioned gaffe.

Multiple Choice

8. Which one are you most likely to do?
    a. Look up words you don't know
    b. Look up pronunciations you don't know
    c. All of the above
    d. None of the above

In the Margins
(For LAF)

GROWING UP, he wasn't much of a reader. Then, inexplicably, as sometimes happens when the book bug bites a would-be bibliophile, he began to read book after book. Even more, he found himself unable to keep himself from engaging in dialogue with these books, filling their margins with his astute observations, affirmations, and even criticisms. No one suspected he'd ever become a writer, let alone a successful novelist. Now these ragged paperbacks, filled with the scrawl of his brilliant mind, are hunted by collectors and studied by the academy, as they ponder how, during his lifetime, he was able to go from the streets to the ivory towers with the ease of something that naturally metamorphoses into a splendidness that transcends our very ability to express beauty.

Memories

A Haiku with a Footnote

No matter what she does or who she's with, she can't forget him*.

---

* She realizes it was only a week of her life, the time when her friend bailed on their vacation at the last minute and she decided to go anyway, against the advice of her sister, who thought it was rather reckless for a Black woman to travel to the Outer Banks on her own, but the cottage had been rented, and she was in need of the sanctity provided by beautiful sunsets off the East Coast. Then she met him. He was struggling to get over a relationship that failed him—one that, as fate would have it, he would later return to in the months to follow—and somehow in the emptiness of time and the hypnotizing way in which the shore yielded to the water, they found themselves in need of each other. She had never felt so connected to a person before, and because of this, she wrestles to find similar satisfaction in the different people she has dated since, thus the point of this poem.

Tiny Umbrella

SHE CARRIES A TINY UMBRELLA, one that fits inside of pretty much anything, and he looks at this umbrella, wondering what purpose it would serve should she find herself standing in a rain shower or the blazing sun, this tiny umbrella that seems like an umbrella in name only, this thing that is more ornamental than utilitarian, and he worries about her and what will happen should she ever need to use this thing, wanting to say something about it to her, a stranger, but he realizes that tiny umbrella is none of his business and his opinion will never be solicited for such a thing, so he reluctantly walks away, trying to draw away any of the natural elements that might one day circumvent that tiny umbrella with him.

The Making of Art

264

HER FILM WAS ONLY one minute, and it didn't win a single award at the festival. However, the making of that same film, a separate documentary she created just for the hell of it, had a running time of nearly half an hour and ended up taking the top prize.

Books Galore (The Alternate Version)

Inspired by Kafka's "The Bridge"

I NOTICED the piles of books stacked against her wall and thought, "What better gift than to make myself into a bookcase?" So I moved the books toward the center of the floor and positioned myself against the wall, arms outstretched, and waited. She stepped over the books, ignoring them, ignoring me, and eventually I cleared my throat to bring my structure to her attention. She sighed and reluctantly began to load my arms, the top of my head, the slant of my back, the up crook of my lifted foot, and pretty soon, the floor was empty of books. As I became a piece of furniture in her room, I waited for her to take at least one book from what had now become an excruciating burden, but she found more interest in her phone. I eventually bowed and collapsed, and the books (and I) lay on the floor to be stepped over for the foreseeable future.

Deja Vu

He has written this poem before. It was so long ago that he'd simply forgotten he'd already written it.

Now, he wonders how he can make this poem different from its predecessor, because no one wants to write the same poem over and over again.

So he starts with his admission of what has happened and hopes the things he's experienced since his first effort have sharpened his understanding of the world around him a bit more, and as result, shaped the poem into something, while similar, still unique enough to be new.

Upon Watching "Boyz N the Hood" for the Umpteenth Time

I WONDER if Tre's real name was Furious Styles III
or if he was just named Tre.

The Space Between Us

THEY WALK SIDE BY SIDE, along the empty city streets, the street lights reflecting off the remains of the earlier shower. Dinner was nice, but not as magical as he'd hoped. He considers reaching across the twelve inches of space that separate them and taking hold of her hand, but he is unsure if she would approve, so he walks beside her, trying to ignore the space between them that grows wider with each step.

Leonora Carrington

269

She would like to believe her artwork was inevitable, but in her mind's quietest moments, she wonders if she would have been the artist she became had not her mother given her the book that taught her to dream while awake.

Sheep

THE SHEEP GATHER in the pasture without the shepherd, their wools fluffed identically with self-applied brands to their hips, bearing the insignia of their shepherd, who has yet to know they actually exist. They graze off the same diet and look at stray sheep in the wilderness as lost. They will stand by until their shepherd calls them to action, at which point they will do whatever he says so the world will know his greatness.

Remedios Varo

She was once torn between whether her nocturnal exploits were dreams or nightmares, but then she came to realize even the worst of her nightmares were still dreams.

Tiptoeing

272

SHE TIPTOES THROUGH HIS THOUGHTS, leaving barely a trace, floating almost imperceptibly, and he must ask himself if she was ever really there at all.

Bridge
A Haiku

I BUILT a bridge with all my words, and I hope it still stands years from now.

'88 to Infinity

ALL I WANTED to do was be funky fresh, with the Coca-Cola sweatshirt, Guess watch, Girbaud jeans, and black cement Jordan 3s, haircut a skin fade with the slanted part in the front center, waves hooked up hard to get the ladies seasick, looking for the house party since J-Cool's parents were away for the weekend. Paris and Devonte were our version of Kid 'N Play, two tall slim brothers sporting the graffiti overalls, one shoulder down, outdancing everyone to the point they could only dance with each other. Quixote on the wheels of steel, periodically beatboxing with the songs, and a gang of brothers rotating through the mic, longing to be the top emcee at Point City High. Me, I was off to the side making sure the wall didn't fall down, had my eye on Felicia, and if all went well, I'd be able to call her later at home from the wall rotary phone in the hall once my folks had gone to bed, cord pulled tightly into the adjacent bathroom so I could have privacy and spit whatever game I could come up with in my deepest voice.

Recess

275

He'd never hit anyone before, always thought his fists too small, his background too soft, but the bully was unrelenting and he'd simply grown tired of running away.

Handholding
A Haiku

HER HAND WAS SOFTER than he had dreamed it would be. He could not let go.

Upon Watching "The Five Heartbeats" for the Umpteenth Time

SURELY, I am not the only one who thought the group might sing at the picnic at the end of the film, as opposed to just dance.

Night Journaling

EVERY NIGHT she scribbles a little bit of her pain onto the pages of her journal, leaving them there in their physical representation, while making space for the joy of her day to radiate freely through her remaining thoughts.

Virginia

Her publisher explained to her that putting a naked woman on the cover would help to sell more books, since this was a poetry collection, after all.

"We can make it tasteful, just part of a breast," her editor said.

"The state of Virginia has a woman's breast exposed," she responded.

"Exactly," said her editor.

The two women continued to discuss book covers and how to sell poetry, knowing somehow the writing was simply not enough.

Yves Klein

Blue extended from the center in every direction until it reached the edges of the canvas, almost pulsing, as if the color had become a living thing and the canvas merely a resting place before it went home with you, neatly tucked into your memory, replaying itself across your mind's eyes, its paintbrush a distant memory, its artist looming somewhere in the distance, somewhere beyond time.

Life

PLEASE TURN to the next page.

Part Eleven

Lycanthropy

WITH THE FULL moon resting outside his bathroom window, he looks into the mirror and shakes (un)controllably, believing he is turning into a werewolf. Saliva rolls over the edges of his teeth as he bends his fingers into a crouching posture and hisses at his reflection, swearing he can feel his ears elongating. He wants to transform into a werewolf so he will be strong and vicious enough to take on his mother's drunken boyfriend. It is impossible for a man to beat up a werewolf, he tells himself, as he snarls and opens the bathroom door.

Death By Hot Wings

MOUTHFUL OF BEE STINGS, milk an imitation salve, scalp sprouting water as if seeping up from a flooded field, the echos of a pain that hovers above me like an open furnace, thoroughly crushing me with its capsaicin, and I did this to myself, to prove to myself, what exactly?

Elle
A Tanka

SHE IS MY AUTUMN, her kisses like Sweetgum leaves waving from above, yellow, auburn, gold, and red, the twilight of perfection.

She

HER POEM IS ABOUT SELF-LOVE, but she doesn't mind that Zora thinks it's about her. Honestly, it could very well be.

Upon Watching "Gravity" for the Umpteenth Time

ONCE SANDRA BULLOCK returned to Earth, she apparently took over George Clooney's role in the *Ocean's Eleven* franchise.

Prose Poetry #2

290

Try as he may to write a poem, his words longed to betray him, their desire for a narrative far too strong to contain. This poem is their compromise.

Banned

The school board in his hometown banned his debut novel, but he still left a copy of it with his hometown public library, the place he'd first fallen in love with reading, the place he once called his personal Fortress of Solitude.

There would be no trace of the book in the library records, but it was still there, waiting to be read by those for whom it was written.

Fairy Tales

292

She slept peacefully as Anita Baker sang her yawns and Greg Phillinganes tickled the ivories until their laughter could be heard from heaven.

Popcorn

Their fingers will touch in the small popcorn bucket, and they will smile. She will then eat a handful and lick the salt and butter from her fingertips before getting more.

For the rest of the afternoon, he will ponder if it is too soon in their relationship for double-dipping.

Diane Franklin

So I GUESS it's safe to say John Cusack was not the
last American virgin.

Reminiscing on Hyperboles

Morgan misses a time when her daughter spoke in hyperboles, and everything was "the greatest thing ever" or "the funniest thing in the world" or something was "*super* awesome." Now her daughter speaks in a different language, one that is abstract and confusing, and prefers to spend time with her friends, who understand this new vocabulary, this younger diction.

Some days Morgan wishes she could take her daughter back to a simpler time, a time when their relationship was the only thing in the world that mattered, the center of each other's universe, but she knows this, too, is hyperbole.

Botany

He has been busy experimenting with various sativa, crossbreeding in a quest to create the best strand the world has ever experienced. If he is lucky, he will not only succeed, but receive an "A" in his sixth grade botany class, as well.

Still

THEY LIE STILL. Red light still. Casket still. He inside of her, their bodies pulsing singularly, their heartbeats trying to keep up. They will move again. Soon. But not yet. The moment is too perfect.

Artificial

THE PLAN WAS to use this new technology to help her when she got writer's block and needed ideas on how to proceed. She delegated a skill she would have normally honed herself, and that began a line of delegations that eventually culminated in her becoming less skilled at the actual craft of writing, while simultaneously developing a mastery of writing prompts for the technology that would eventually replace her altogether.

The Heights of Our Dreams

Sometimes he dreams he is lying on the top bunk of a bed that is delicately balanced on the precipice of a mountain, the moon seemingly a stone's throw away. He wants to rise but doesn't trust his balance, and his fear of falling licks at his nerves like live wires dancing near water. He does not want to lie there, but lie there he must, because his fear is manageable when he motionless, his dream almost feeling like a dream. He will awake relieved, yet tired, feeling a part of him was left in his dream and that part of him is still paralyzed with fear.

Memories of a Broken Heart

THERE ARE moments when they remember him and feel a pang of regret. It would have never worked, they know, but he had loved them so fiercely, the type of love they had always craved—the kind of love they still crave—but just not from him. This is why their heart is aching, not from longing, but from the feeling he deserved better, something far greater than they could have ever given him in this lifetime.

Good Storytelling

W‍HAT IS GOOD STORYTELLING?

It's when you can have Tom Cruise kill a samurai, then get captured by the other samurai, wind up becoming friends with his captors, start a relationship with the wife of the samurai he killed, learn the samurai ways and their language (and apparently rise up the ranks), earn their respect, fight against his former employers while wearing the *yoroi* of the samurai he killed, and survive to be the "last" of the samurai.

You know what you are seeing is the classic "white savior" archetype, but you accept it. Why?

Because the storytelling is so good.

One Man's Opinion

The governor spoke in superlatives, as he was wont to do, everything he touched being "the best the state had seen in years." If he were to evaluate his term, he would have given himself the highest marks possible. The scholars from the various political science departments across the state, though, in an impartial study put together by an external consulting firm, deemed him to be the worst governor since Reconstruction. The governor's team felt there was much to learn—to understand— about the study's results, but the governor held fast to the idea his governing was beyond reproach, that the study had been orchestrated by his political enemies, and that he was indeed as amazing as he had always believed himself to be.

The Woman They Found

Her lips are electric blue like animated lightning, her eyes onyx, the blackness squeezing out what remains of the white, her fingertips dark with soil, her face pale as limestone. They have found her here, just beyond the headstones, interred in the crisp moonlit air of night. They touch her chest, feel for breaths that have long since evaporated, and ponder how she arrived at this place. Had she crawled up from an open plot, or was she returning to one? They sit with her until dawn, when the last of them falls asleep and she vanishes into their memories.

The Books of Summer

Her summer is filled with books, ones she has collected over the past year for this special occasion. This is her reward for an exhausting school year. Now she can sit on the porch of the remodeled antebellum house she and her husband bought after he made partner. Just the books and the breeze, her feet dangling off the porch swing, an Arnold Palmer sitting close by, the shade of the old oak in the front yard shielding her from the blaze of an apathetic sun.

Fermi's Paradox

WHILE STARING AT THE BRILLIANT, endless night sky, Enrico noticed a star that seemed to be moving closer and closer. He'd once asked the question "Where is everybody?"

Now he had his answer.

Musing

AT WHAT POINT does musing become a poem and that poem then become a story? Is a plot implied, insinuated with the musing, since the musing clearly comes from a predefined context? If the reader is not privy to that context, does this negate the story's ability to exist as a story? If I am the one musing, thereby making me the protagonist, do my efforts to manage my musing upon the page constitute an internal conflict and, therefore, provide what many scholars would identify as a plot, thereby making this a story or, at minimum, a narrative poem and not a musing? If you are reading this, do you think it even matters?

Vocabulary

The vocabulary they developed over their time together is what she misses most. He was the only person with whom she could speak it, so in losing him, she has lost those words, as well.

Open Window

In the winter, she likes to sleep with the window open, against the wishes of her wife.

- What if something were to come into the house—God forbid a person?

- It's a both a reasonable concern and a reasonable risk.

- How can it be both?

- I am willing to take the risk, but I understand your concern.

They are at a stalemate, or so it appears, but as the first sentence of this story suggests, this is a regular occurrence, and this argument, if you were so inclined to call it one, is part of a routine, because the window will always be open in the winter, and her wife will always express her concern for such an action.

Forgiveness
A Haiku

HE HAS CHOSEN to forgive her, but she has not forgiven herself.

Part Twelve

The Toy Box

Sometimes they felt like they were toys of the gods, those who strutted about the heavens moving them around into various chaotic and perilous predicaments. It seemed as though, but for the circumstances of fate, they might have been gods themselves. Maybe they would have been more benevolent in those roles—at least they preferred to believe they would.

In reality, they were left to the whims of those who, at times, showed little signs of empathy and preferred random conflict supplied by hubristic hypotheses.

They were toys, a source of amusement, and their world was neatly ensconced in a box, the whole of which sat in a single file on the gods' hard drive.

Same Story, Different Day

SHE HAS PUBLISHED the same novel five times, each version vastly different from the previous one. The title, though, is the same, although there is information about the edition number in the subtitle. Fans of her work know she will only write one story during her lifetime, but they are awestruck by how many different ways she can write it.

My Grandmother, the Thesaurus

SHORTLY AFTER MY little sister left with her boyfriend for the prom, my grandmother remarked, "That boy shole is strong in the face!"

"What does that mean?" I asked.

"He don't favor nobody."

I shrugged.

"He look like he fell out of the ugly tree and hit every branch on the way to the ground."

"Oh. I get it."

"Boy, don't tell me your elevator is stuck between floors."

"Huh?"

"You ain't the sharpest knife in the drawer, is you?"

"What do you mean?" I asked.

"Ain't the brightest crayon in the box."

I didn't know how to respond, so I said, "I'm good."

"I just hope they ain't too serious. We don't need no little monsters running around here."

I nodded, not entirely sure what she meant by

any of this, but guessing that whatever it was, it wasn't entirely good.

Ninja, Please!
After CM

THE SONGSTRESS, after years of searching for love, found it in the arms of an actor, and when she did, she wrote and recorded a song expressing her love and devotion toward this new muse.

That song became a hit with her fans.

Years later, that relationship ended on a sour note, and she felt the need to write and record yet another song, detailing her anger and disgust with him.

Needless to say, that song, too, became a hit with her fans.

Privacy

THE TAXI CAB cruised along the George Washington Bridge, as the couple snuggled in the backseat. She touched him discreetly, massaging him slowly. He draped his arm around her shoulder in response and leaned in, tugging gently on her earlobe with his teeth. The taxi driver chuckled to himself and stared out into the night at the glowing skyline.

Tik Tok and You Don't Stop

Yes, I am the creator of that short video, the one that misspells "You're" with "your" or "hear" with "here." I am the one who pastes unnecessary words from the description in an enormous font across the key action of the video. I am the one who does my own closed captioning with the wrong words. I am the one who posts the "Oh no no no" laughing audio track to everything I do. I am the one who makes people copy other people's funny videos and try to pass them off as their own. I am the one who makes people risk their lives trying to pull off pranks. I am the one who comes up with bad choreography so I can show you my fifty-eleven children messing it up. Yes, I am responsible for eating up hours out of your day.

You are welcome.

Summer Night Swings

BACK WHEN THEY WERE KIDS, the two of them would swing together, her seated on his lap facing him, as they moved back and forth in tandem. If you lived in Marvin Groves, this was the way you communicated to everyone you were a couple. Occasionally he would try to kiss her, but she would remind him she was saving herself for marriage. So they just enjoyed swinging.

Nighttime in the City

THE CITY HELD many soundtracks in its palms, songs and whispers from disparate lovers, tickling its skin and radiating out through its fingers into the Hudson like eight million shadows of the Supreme.

My Life in the Sunshine

322

Roy borrowed the sun from Apollo and, with his glowing mallets, struck his vibraphone so we could dance and sing of bees and things and flowers.

Quotes

I HAVE a book of quotes on my desk, and after reading bits and pieces of wisdom over the years, I have come to question a few things. For example, was the person who espoused the quote really all that wise? A broken clock is right twice a day, and even a toddler can utter something that strikes us in our philosophic core. Secondly, and more importantly, did the person even say that? Not so much did they say it, but did the statement originate with them when they said it? There are countless times when someone famous quoted a line from an obscure poet and got all the credit.

So maybe this book of quotes reminds me if any of my works take on a life of their own, I will recognize success by way of seeing it quoted—and likely attributed to someone else.

Morning Writing
A Haiku

WHILE SHE HATES READING HAIKU, she usually writes one each morning.

What's a Long Shot to a Sharp Shooter?

After Phonte

THERE WAS nothing spectacular about him. He wasn't an athlete or a scholar. He wasn't gifted in music and was too much of a minimalist to make any kind of fashion statement. He might've thought of himself as ordinary, except for the fact he harbored something even his more accomplished peers failed to have in any meaningful way: confidence. That is why Johnny Townsend had no trouble walking up to Sharonda Wilson, the presumptive homecoming queen, and asking her to prom.

Puppy

Dog bowl - $15
    Collar - $30
    Dog Shampoo - $8.50
    Dog Bed - $100
    Harness - $50
    Lead - $15
    Toys - $10
    Dog poo bags - $15
    Puppy pads - $40
    Dog Food - $100
    Treats - $15
    First Aid Kit - $30
    A daughter's happiness: Priceless

Eyes Closed
A Haiku

IF I MEDITATE LONG ENOUGH, my thoughts become a stream of prayers.

Love Is More Than a Four-Letter Word

THEIR GRANDMOTHER still trips up on their pronouns, but it is not intentional or spiteful. She just needs a little more time to form the habit so her language is fluid. She will not give up, though, because she loves them too much to quit trying.

What Poetry Is Not

The professor told them not to write cryptic poems just to leave the reader asking questions. He said poetry was not some kind of game of verbal gymnastics, some form of intellectual masturbation, an escape room designed by an obnoxious guy named Jay, a forced contest to read another's mind and know exactly what kind of birthday gift she really wanted, and other examples that flew well over his students' heads and did little to reinforce his point.

The Circle

THE ROOM IS A CIRCLE, and the circle is spinning, and the people within the room live on sides of the circle, and occasionally they move their things from one side to the other, and they do their best to get along, though, at times, they grow to despise each other and quarrel—even hate each other— and wish they were not in the same circle, but they are, and they will continue spinning in this circle and moving in this circle, until the circle ceases to spin and they fly out into the nothingness from which the circle has been shielding them this entire time.

Commas

SHE HAS OBSERVED HOW many commas he uses in his writing and has vowed to increase the number of commas in her own writing. She's wrestled with how to use that punctuation mark correctly in her own writing for years, so she figures by adopting his writing style, she will learn to better control her usage of it, never once asking herself if this esteemed writer, on whom she has based her decision, uses commas properly in his own writing.

What the Author Tells Himself
A Haiku

IF HIS BOOK had French flaps, surely it would fly off all the bookstore shelves.

A Moment

Don't leave, she whispers, as he sits on the edge of the bed, contemplating the work day ahead. He does not want to leave her—can still feel the heat of her body from beneath the sheets—and decides to return to her. If this is a test to see if he will do what needs to be done to take care of them both, he has failed. If it is not a test, but a moment, one that he will reflect over fondly in his later years when he re-examines the various magical moments of his life, he has made the right decision. In this moment, though, he does not know if it is either, nor is he particularly concerned.

Ironies of the Writing Life

SHE USED to get on his case about his writing erotic stories, claiming that's all he could write. Her words bruised his ego, so he started working on his writing by reading and studying more literature. In the end, he ended up writing stories that were completely arcane in a literary form that was entirely unpopular, and she, well, she became famous for writing erotica.

I Hate Your Doppelgängers, Too

SHE HATES him because he looks like someone who once hurt her. He has not yet spoken to her, has not gotten beyond making eye contact, but she will have none of it. She knows it is not his fault, though. (Who can control their genes?) Still, she knows what he will say, how he will laugh, how he will feel inside of her, how he will one day break her heart, and she has no bandwidth for him or anyone who looks like him.

Short

He loves when she writes short.

He's not as much a fan when she writes long.

It's not that she is completely incapable of writing the longer form.

It's that her content works better when written in a short form.

It's like a person who made an decent LP when they could have easily made a great EP.

Chaucer

WHEN THAT APRIL with its sweet showers, the drought of March hath pierced to the root.

If only his Chaucer class had been required to memorize that version, but his professor relished seeing her students stand in front of the class, one by one, and do their best Middle English accent.

Years later, the students would spit those memorized passages to impress their children and show the value of a liberal arts education.

Parting Thoughts

As SHE LIES on her deathbed, afraid and confused, a melody slowly works its way up her throat and onto her lips, and as she sings it in that final moment, she remembers having loved and been loved fiercely and unconditionally.

Acknowledgments

Thank you to my wife and daughter, my parents, my brother and his family, my wife's family, my fellow writers, my colleagues, my students, and those who have supported me on this strange and interesting creative journey.

About the Author

Ran Walker (he/him) is the author of over 30 books. His short stories, flash fiction, microfiction, and poetry have appeared in a variety of anthologies and journals. Prior to becoming a writer and educator, he worked in magazine publishing and practiced law in Mississippi.

He is the winner of the Indie Author Project's 2019 National Indie Author of the Year Award, the 2019 Black Caucus of the American Library Association Best Fiction Ebook Award, the 2018 Virginia Indie Author Project Award for Adult Fiction, and the 2021 Blind Corner Afrofuturism Microfiction Contest. Ran is an Associate Professor of English and Creative Writing at Hampton University and teaches with Writer's Digest University. He lives in Virginia with his wife and much better half, Lauren, and his amazing daughter, Zoë.

Also by Ran Walker

B-Sides and Remixes

30 Love: A Novel

Mojo's Guitar: A Novel/ (Il était une fois Morris Jones)

Afro Nerd in Love: A Novella

The Keys of My Soul: A Novel

The Race of Races: A Novel

The Illest: A Novella

Bessie, Bop, or Bach: Collected Stories

Four Floors (with Sabin Prentis)

Black Hand Side: Stories

White Pages: A Novel

She Lives in My Lap

Reverb

Work-In-Progress

Daykeeper

Most of My Heroes Don't Appear On No Stamps

Portable Black Magic: Tales of the Afro Strange

The Strange Museum: 50-Word Stories

Bees + Things + Flowers: Microfictions

The World Is Yours: Microfictions

Can I Kick It?: Sneaker Microfiction and Poetry (with Van Garrett)

The Golden Book: A 50-Year Marriage Told In 50-Word Stories